MR. MAGORIUM'S WONDER EMPORIUM

A Little Magic

By Gail Herman

Based on the motion picture written
and directed by Zach Helm

Scholastic Inc.

New York   Toronto   London   Auckland   Sydney
Mexico City   New Delhi   Hong Kong   Buenos Aires

ANYTHING CAN HAPPEN!

walden.com/magorium and **magorium.com**

ISBN-13: 978-0-439-91249-5
ISBN-10: 0-439-91249-0

 WALDEN MEDIA™

This book is published in cooperation with Walden Media, LLC.
Walden Media and the Walden Media skipping stone logo are trademarks and registered trademarks of
Walden Media, LLC, 294 Washington Street, Boston, Massachusetts 02108.

Published by Scholastic Inc. All rights reserved.
SCHOLASTIC and associated logos are trademarks and/or registered trademarks of Scholastic Inc.

12 11 10 9 8 7 6 5 4 3 2 1   7 8 9 10 11 12/0

Printed in the U.S.A.
First printing, October 2007

It was still summer.
But Eric Appelbaum wasn't in camp.
He didn't like camp.
He didn't have friends there.
In fact, Eric didn't have friends at all.

"I let you stay home," Eric's mom said to him. "But you need to make one friend this summer."

Eric wanted to make friends.

He just didn't know how.

Not even when he was at his favorite place—Mr. Magorium's Wonder Emporium.

At the store, the morning started out like any other.

Airplanes flew and balls bounced all by themselves.

It was a toy store filled with magic, thanks to Mr. Magorium.

Eric knew Mr. Magorium was magic.
And his assistant, Molly Mahoney?
Eric thought she was magic, too.
Only she didn't know it.
And maybe, just maybe, Eric had
a little bit of magic himself.

Eric liked Mr. Magorium and
Mahoney a lot.
But things were changing.
He heard Mr. Magorium say
something about going away.

Then Henry Weston came to work at the store.

Henry knew about money.

But he didn't know about magic.

One day Eric saw something strange at the store.

Everything in one corner turned a dull, dull gray.

All the color had disappeared!

"We need to keep an eye on this," Mr. Magorium said.

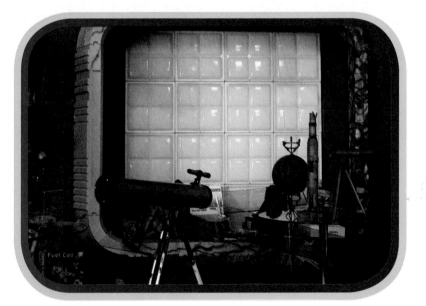

The next day, Eric checked the spot.
Still gray.

Then he stopped by the building logs.
Eric began to build something
different—all by himself, as usual.

There! He was done.

A giant statue of Abraham Lincoln stood on the floor.

"Who helped you?" asked Henry.

"Nobody," said Eric.

At home, Eric's mom asked, "Did you play with anyone today?"

Eric shook his head.

"You can do it," she told him. "Start by saying hi."

The next day Eric went to
Henry's office.

He held up a sign that said: "Hi."

Henry held up a sign, too. "Hi."
But he couldn't come out to play.
"I NEVER STOP WORKING,"
he wrote.

At the store, the gray was
spreading farther and farther. . . .

Then one day it got worse.
The toys were out of control!

Mr. Magorium called a meeting.

"The store is upset because I'm leaving," he told Eric, Mahoney, and Henry.

"But don't worry. Mahoney will take over."

Only Mahoney wasn't sure that she could.

Mr. Magorium wasn't just going away.
He was dying.
Mahoney rushed him to the hospital.

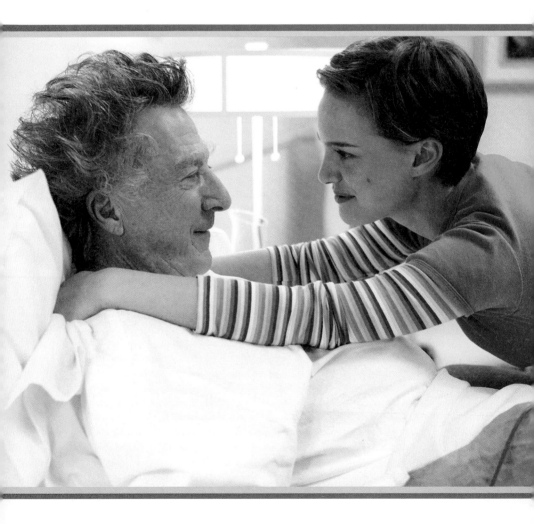

Eric went to visit him.
He brought lots of presents.
But he knew nothing would help.
Mr. Magorium was 242 years old.
It was his time.

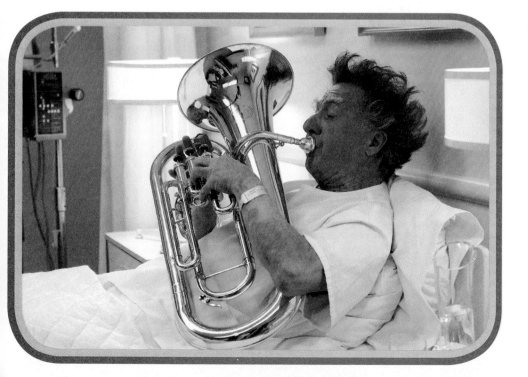

That night, Eric showed Henry
his hat collection.
Henry put on a silly one.
He spoke in a funny voice.
Henry Weston was playing!
And Eric had made a friend!

The next few days were very sad.

Mr. Magorium was gone.

Hundreds of people came to his funeral.

Mr. Magorium had many friends.

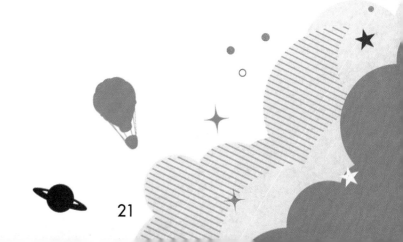

After the funeral, the store turned gray. Every inch.

"It just needs a little magic," Eric said.

"I don't have any magic," Mahoney said. "I have to sell the store."

That can't happen! Eric thought.
The store is too important.
Eric went to see Henry.
"I want to buy the store," he said.
"I can pay two hundred thirty-seven dollars in pennies, nickels, and dimes."

Henry talked to Mahoney.

All the while, she stared at a block of wood.

Mr. Magorium had given it to her.

She knew it held some sort of secret.

"Do you believe it's magic?" Henry asked.

Mahoney thought of Mr. Magorium. She did believe it. She did! The block of wood flipped. It jumped and soared. Mahoney knew there was magic inside it.

It was in the middle of the night, but Mahoney wanted to talk to Eric about the store.

"Maybe it just needs someone to believe in it," she said. "Someone who never believed in anything before."

The next morning, Mahoney rushed to the store to test out her plan. Henry had fallen asleep there.

"Do you think this store is magic?" she asked.

"Of course," he said. "But it's not just the store. It's you."

28

Mahoney needed to believe in her own magic.

She raised her arms and suddenly the toy instruments played.

Balls bounced. Airplanes flew.

The store burst into color.
The magic was back!

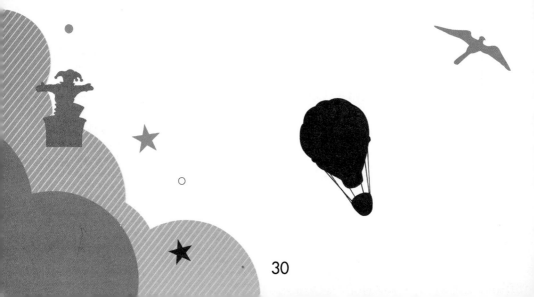

Eric, Mahoney, and Henry hugged.
Mahoney would never sell now.
The store was saved!